Molly Gets
MAD

Suzy Kline

Molly Gets
MAD

Illustrated by **Diana Cain Bluthenthal**

G. P. Putnam's Sons • New York

As always, special appreciation for
my editor, Anne O'Connell

Library of Congress Cataloging-in-Publication Data
Kline, Suzy. Molly gets mad / Suzy Kline ;
illustrated by Diana Cain Bluthenthal.
p. cm. Summary: Third grader Molly is jealous of Florence's
superior ice skating ability but makes an interesting discovery
about teamwork when she joins the hockey team.
[1. Jealousy—Fiction. 2. Sportsmanship—Fiction. 3. Ice skating—Fiction.
4. Hockey—Fiction. 5. Schools—Fiction.] I. Bluthenthal, Diana Cain, ill.
II. Title. PZ7.K6797 Ml 2001 [Fic]—dc21 00-062672 ISBN 0-399-23408-X
1 3 5 7 9 10 8 6 4 2
First Impression

Contents

1

Mysterious Beginning

It was 3:07 P.M. when the YMCA-bus bell rang at North School.

Brrrrrrring!

"Hey, Molly!" I called, whipping on my Yankees baseball cap. "That's us! Time to go on our secret YMCA field trip."

"Wait a minute, Morty," she replied. "I have to shoot my basketball into the garbage can first."

Plunk!

"Two points!" Molly yelled, holding up both hands.

Mr. Yarg, our third-grade teacher, came racing over. "That's a technical foul."

"Ooops!" Molly replied. When she took the ball out of the garbage can, a banana peel and a wad of masking tape were sitting on top.

Florence giggled. It looked like the basketball had a hairdo.

Mr. Yarg wasn't laughing. He was pointing his finger at Molly. "How many times have I told you not to throw a ball in the room?"

Molly's eyeballs went around like two Ferris wheels. She couldn't come up with an exact number.

"Well," Mr. Yarg barked, "this time I'm keeping it overnight."

"But . . . that's my Rebecca Lobo basketball! It was my favorite Christmas present."

"Too bad, Molly," Mr. Yarg replied, putting it in his teacher's cabinet and closing the door.

"Come on," I yelled. "We gotta go!"

Molly grabbed her backpack and stormed out of the room. When we sat down on the bus, I warned her, "You better cool it, Molly. Mr. Yarg wasn't joking around. You didn't even say you were sorry."

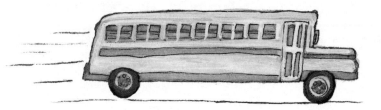

"Morty," she sighed, "you sound like you're forty." Then she grinned. "Hey, that rhymes . . . Forty Morty!"

"That's so funny I forgot to laugh," I snapped.

"There's still time," Molly said.

When I shot Molly a *T. rex* look, she stopped bugging me.

"Okay, Mort. I don't appreciate being laughed at either." Then she turned and glared at Florence, who was the one who laughed about the banana ball.

Florence was the new girl who came to our class last month. She carried a purple backpack and was very quiet.

Molly sank down in her seat and lowered her voice. "Promise you won't tell anyone?"

I pulled my earlobes twice. That was our secret code for "I'll keep it a secret."

"I *have* to practice my shooting. I want to be a great basketball player and make the most points like my sister in high school."

"You mean you have to be the top dog," I answered. "That's no secret. I've known that since kindergarten. If we played Duck, Duck, Goose, you had to be 'it.' In Seven Up, you had to be 'up.' "

Molly nodded. "Yeah, but we don't play those games anymore."

"No. Now it's baseball, and you have to score the most runs, or in soccer or hockey, the most goals. If we race, you have to come in—"

"First," Molly agreed. "I also *have* to have the most loyal friend in the world—and that's you!" When she held up two fingers, I got her message. It was our secret code for "good going."

But I didn't feel like holding up two fingers. Calling me Forty Morty was *not* my idea of good going.

Just at that moment, Aya leaned over the back of our seat. "So, did you guys figure out where we're going today on our secret field trip?"

"Nope," I said. "Don't you know?" Aya was like the third-grade detective. She usually knew everything.

Aya shook her head. "No, I bugged my mom all last night. She refused to tell me anything. Just that we needed permission slips, that it was ten minutes out of town and that it was going to be lots of fun."

"Whoa," I said. Quickly I checked my back jeans pocket to see if I had my permission slip. Yup, it was there.

Slowly, Aya lowered her voice. "Speaking

of mysteries, I know another one. It's about Florence."

Molly immediately turned around and looked up at Aya. "What mystery?"

Aya began her story. "You know I got a new kitty named Ginger."

"Yeah," we answered.

"Well, for the last week she's been jumping up on my bed at six-fifteen in the morning and waking me up. I know the time because I check my digital clock."

"I thought this mystery was about Florence," I complained.

"It *is*," Aya insisted. "The first time it happened I was sitting in bed petting Ginger. Suddenly, I heard a noise from across the street. I went to the window to see what it was." Aya paused. "It was Florence's station wagon backing out of the driveway. Florence came running out of the house and got inside. She had her backpack with her."

"Where was she going?" we both asked.

"*That's* the mystery," Aya replied. "So I checked the next morning and the next. Florence and her mother did the same thing. In fact, they left early this morning, too. But this time her backpack was really bulging."

"Hmmm!" Molly wondered as she looked over at Florence. Her red bushy hair was tied up in a scrunchie. She was still reading. Her purple backpack took up most of her seat.

Vincenzo was just leaning over the aisle. "Hey, Flo," he called, "do you know where this bus is taking us?"

Molly laughed. "That's a dumb question," she whispered. "She'd be the last person to know that."

But we watched and waited for Florence's answer just the same.

"Yes," Florence said, nodding. "I do know where we're going."

My eyes almost popped out of their sockets. The three of us said it together . . .

"SHE KNOWS?"

2
The Mystery Place

"Where *are* we going?" I asked Florence.

"It's a secret. The only reason I know is because my mother helped organize it. I don't want to spoil the surprise for you."

We all stared at Florence's purple backpack.

Aya didn't waste any time. "What's in your purple backpack?" she asked. "It's really bulging!"

Florence smiled. "You'll find out later. I always keep them with me on special days like today. For good luck."

"*Them?*" Aya asked.

Molly leaned forward. "*You're* part of the surprise?"

Now Florence was the center of attention. The people around her were all listening.

"Kind of," she replied.

Molly folded her arms and fumed.

When we drove by Frogs' Pond, everyone pointed and cheered at the kids skating there. But Molly didn't. She looked away and frowned.

"You're *still* mad at her for laughing?" I asked.

Molly finally spit it out. "Florence only made three points last month in basketball. I don't know why she comes to these YMCA sports programs. She's no athlete. But *she's* the only one who knows about the secret field trip. She's even part of the secret. It's not fair that Florence knows and we don't. It makes me mad!"

I hoped Florence didn't read lips. She was looking back at us with a worried look.

"Hey!" Aya said. "My watch says ten minutes have passed. We should be getting to the mystery place any second now."

Vincenzo pressed his nose against the window. "I wish we were going to San Francisco to see the Forty-niners!" he said. "They almost won the Super Bowl this year!"

When the bus driver took a right off the road onto a long driveway, we saw a dark aluminum building.

It looked like a steel armadillo.

14

"Hey!" Vincenzo shouted. "It's almost as big as a FOOTBALL FIELD!"

Aya stood up in the bus. "So . . . what is it?" she demanded.

3
Two Surprises

"It's the new ice rink," Florence answered softly.

"OH, YEAH!"
Vincenzo boomed.
"It just opened up last month. I've never been yet. Has anyone else?"

I shook my head.
"Not me. Wow . . . we're going skating in the brand-new rink! That *is* a surprise!"

Mr. Williams, our teacher at the Y, was waiting for us at the door. He jumped on the bus. "Welcome, kids!" he said, adjusting his Boston Red Sox cap. "This week we're going to work on our skating skills. I know most of you skate regularly at Frogs' Pond, but starting today, you'll get a chance to skate in a real rink. Our town finally got one!"

Everyone cheered and clapped.

Molly grinned. "I haven't seen Florence at the pond once this winter. I bet she's going to fall a lot today!"

A blonde-haired lady stepped onto the bus. She was wearing a jacket that said *Hilltop Ice Rink*.

Mr. Williams introduced her. "Boys and girls, this is Florence's mother, Mrs. Auchinschloss. She owns this new ice rink. We appreciate her invitation to come here."

Mrs. Auchinschloss smiled and waved at Florence. Then she spoke to us. "Please call me Mrs. A. I hope your parents bring you back for more visits, and maybe consider your playing on one of our hockey teams. They're just starting up this Saturday. The youngest players are on the Mites. Depending on your age, you can join the Squirts, Pee Wees, Bantams or Midgets. But you'll *all* be Hilltop Flyers!"

"Which group is for the eight- and nine-year-olds?" Vincenzo asked.

"That would be the Squirts," Mrs. A replied.

"Hey!" Molly said, slapping me five. "That's us! Let's ask our parents if we can join!"

"All right!" I said, slapping her five back.

"Let's get inside and have some fun," Mrs. A said. "Just go over to the front desk and pick out your skates! No charge today."

"Yahoo!" I said. "It's free!"

As soon as we stepped inside the rink, we could see and hear the big Zamboni brushing off the top of the ice. When the blue-and-white truck made its final sweep, the ice looked as clear as an oval mirror.

"What size, kids?" a tall man in a white shirt asked behind the front counter. There must have been a hundred skates hanging on the racks behind him.

Within the next five minutes, we were all taking off our shoes and lacing up our skates.

"I got the last blue pair," Aya bragged.

Molly made a double knot. "The hockey pros wear dark skates, so I wanted brown ones."

"Me, too," I said.

When we looked over, we saw Florence sitting on the bench taking something out of her backpack.

Red skates.

"You have red ones?" Molly said.

"I thought the rental skates were just blue or brown."

"These are my own special pair," Florence said, carrying them into the girls' dressing room.

Molly leaned against the clear plastic

wall that surrounded the rink. "I don't believe it," she said.

"So that's what was making the huge bulge in her purple backpack. Her red skates!" Aya added.

Five minutes later, Mr. Williams called everyone over to the wide wooden bleachers where the spectators sat. "Okay, kids, have a seat. I have another surprise for you."

Another surprise? I thought. *What could that be?*

It turned out to be the biggest surprise of all!

4
The Second Surprise

"Music, please!" Mrs. A called out.

When the loudspeakers came on, I didn't recognize the song. It reminded me of a waltz I had heard once in a bookstore.

Suddenly, Florence appeared on the ice! She was wearing a red sequined ballet dress that matched her red skates.

Everyone gasped!

Molly's jaw dropped.

Florence was in the spotlight!

Her head was down, and her skates
were still. She was waiting for just the right
moment to start.

No one said a word.

Then, Florence started skating very quickly. Her red bushy ponytail flopped behind her. The sequins on her dress sparkled under the lights.

She moved so gracefully! I couldn't believe it. Molly's mouth was wide open the whole time.

When the music reached a certain beat, Florence leaped in the air and landed without falling. Her next move was skating backwards.

It looked like she was having fun, because she smiled so much! "Wow!" I said. "She's spectacular!"

Spectacular.

That word hit Molly's ears like a flying hockey puck. Her tone of voice turned razor-sharp. "So, Miss La-di-da can skate. Big deal."

I looked at her. "Molly Zander! You're jealous of Florence Auchinschloss!"

"No, I'm not!"

"Yes, you are!" I said.

"I wonder when she practices," Vincenzo said. "You gotta practice regularly to skate like that. Look how often the Forty-niners practice."

Aya clicked her fingers. "That's it! *That's* what she's doing early every morning. Practicing at the rink!"

After Florence leaped in the air for the last time, she began twirling around and around and around.

She looked like water going down the bathtub drain.

A perfect red tornado!

We clapped as she made herself smaller and smaller into a tight ball that was practically sitting on the ice. When the music stopped, she stood tall and bowed her head.

"BRAVO!" Mr. Williams shouted as he jumped to his feet. No one had ever heard him say that word before.

"BRAVO!" some of us repeated.

Molly didn't even clap. She just frowned.

I turned and snarled at her, "Don't be such a party pooper!" That's what my dad called me sometimes when I didn't want to do something.

Molly looked me square in the face. "Morty Hill," she said, "I am *not* a party pooper."

Then she stomped off while everyone was still clapping. I just shook my head.

She *was* acting like a party pooper.

"So," Mr. Williams said, "now that we're all inspired, let's go get on the ice and skate ourselves!"

Everyone hopped off the bench and joined Florence. Everyone except Molly. She was sitting in the first row of the bleachers, sulking. I couldn't believe it.

"What's wrong with her?" Aya asked. "Molly's not coming?"

"Nope," I said. "She's just mad . . . Mad Molly!"

5
The Worst Thing

We were skating around the rink for the third time with Florence when Molly finally decided to join us. "Anyone want to have a race?" she asked in a sticky-sweet voice.

Oh no, I thought. I knew what she was up to.

Aya shook her head. "I don't like races."

"Florence?" Molly purred back. "Want to see who's the fastest?"

"I'd rather not," Florence said.

Molly got a long face. I could tell she wanted to show everyone she was still the top dog.

"Count me out," Vincenzo said. "I'm no match for you, Molly." Then he skated over to the sidelines.

"You mean no one will race me?" Molly pleaded.

I gritted my teeth. I wanted to. I wanted to beat her bad and show her a thing or two. But I knew she was faster at Frogs' Pond.

"Not even you, Morty?" Molly asked.

I hemmed and hawed. "Eh . . . I don't think so."

Then she said something that really made *me* mad. "Oh, Forty Morty! You're acting like an old man again."

That did it! She had been pushing my buttons all day. This was the last one. I was going to beat her if it killed me.

I drew a starting line with the blade of my brown skate. "Move over, Molly. I'll race you to the wall and . . . win!"

Molly laughed.

Everyone else moved back or over to the side to watch. Vincenzo cleared his voice from the sidelines. "I'll call."

Molly and I waited.

"Get ready," he called.

We were ready.

"On your mark."

Molly leaned forward with her body.

I leaned forward with mine.

"Get set."

Molly moved her elbows high, ready to swing back and forth.

I looked straight ahead.

"GO!"

We both took off like Olympic athletes. Each of us moved our skates in precision.

Left, right, left, right.

Swish! Swish!

Swish! Swish!

When Molly started to pass me up, her black braids slapped my face. Ouch! *I can't do this,* I thought. My legs were starting to ache as I tried to keep up with her. What was I doing in a race like this?

Then, I heard the cheering and the chanting.

"GO MORTY! GO MORTY!" they yelled. The kids wanted me, the underdog, to win. Not Molly, the top dog. Me!

Suddenly I felt like an engine that just

got a new tankful of gas.

SHWOOOSH!

I skated right up to Molly.

"GO MORTY!" everyone chanted louder and louder.

We skated together side by side.

It was flying time!

"HEY, YOU TWO!" Mr. Williams yelled. "BE CAREFUL!"

I paid no attention to my coach. All I could hear was a voice inside my head that said, *BEAT MOLLY!*

Just as I inched ahead, Molly started swinging her elbows back and forth to gain

more wind speed. One of them hit me on the arm and knocked me off balance.

I went flying through the air.

SPLAT!

I landed on the hard, cold ice on my left ankle.

"Ooooooh!" I groaned as I slid across the rink.

Florence and everyone else came skating over to me. "Are you okay?" she asked.

Molly was so busy racing, she didn't even know what happened. "I WON!" she called, bumping into the plastic wall with a wham and a rattle.

It was kind of sad.

Her big moment and no one cared.

Everyone was gathering around me, the loser.

When Molly finally turned around and noticed, she looked horrified. Quickly, she skated back and joined the others.

I really don't remember much else. My head was spinning and people's faces were starting to blur.

I remember hearing Florence wheezing. I think she skated off to get her inhaler.

Mr. Williams and Mrs. A rushed over. The next thing I knew, I was in the emergency room with my parents, getting an X ray. A little later I found out I had a broken bone in my ankle.

"There goes my hockey season at the Y," I moaned, and all because of *her*.

Mad Molly!

6
Poems and Pain

It's amazing how a pair of crutches can change your life. Thursday, I came to school with a cast covering my foot to my knee. I could wiggle my toes, but that was all. I couldn't walk to school anymore. Mom drove me and helped me hop up the stairs to my third-grade classroom. Too bad our school didn't have an elevator. It would have been cool to ride in it.

"Well, partner," Mr. Yarg said when he

greeted me and Mom at the door. "The frogs and I have missed you."

I smiled. Then Mom asked a favor.

"I'm hoping Morty can eat in the room. It's awfully hard for him to get up and down the stairs."

"I can arrange that, Mrs. Hill. We're glad to have Morty back. We'll take good care of him."

Mom smiled and waved good-bye. "I'll pick you up ten minutes before the last bell, Morty. That way we'll get down the stairs safely before all the children are dismissed. Have a good day!"

When she saw Molly stepping into the room, Mom gave her a hug. "I know you didn't mean any harm. You and Morty are lifelong friends," she said.

"I hope so," Molly said in soft voice.

I didn't look at Molly. Mom knew we hadn't spoken since the accident. I didn't even open up her card. Mom did. She put it up with the others on my bulletin board at home.

I hobbled over to my desk and sat down. Mr. Yarg took my crutches and stacked them against the wall. "I'll get out the rainbow markers," he said. "We can have our first writing assignment on your cast. Roll up your pant leg, Morty."

When I laughed, it felt good. I was glad to be back.

"Okay!" Mr. Yarg joked as he picked up purple and green Magic Markers. "My creative juices are flowing."

First he drew a happy face with green curly hair. Then he wrote . . .

MORTY,
TOUGH BREAK!
MR. YARG

When Florence and Aya came over next to take a turn, Molly watched. While Aya was writing, Florence shared some exciting news. "My mom said you could help me keep the charts for the hockey team on Saturday mornings . . . if you don't mind sitting on the bench."

"I don't mind, Florence. It's something to do."

Molly got a long face.

She was obviously still in the jealous mode. Then Florence wrote something on my cast with a red Magic Marker.

Morty skates
On ice
Real nice
Time will heal your pain
You'll be back on the ice again.
☺-F.A.

Aya read aloud what Florence wrote. "That's beautiful. What do you call that kind of poem, where the first letter of each line spells something out?"

"An acrostic. I love writing them," Florence said. "You pick a topic and write about it. Kind of like a theme. Mine was Morty."

"Gee, thanks, Florence. That's a great poem," I said.

Molly grabbed a Magic Marker. "I can write one, too."

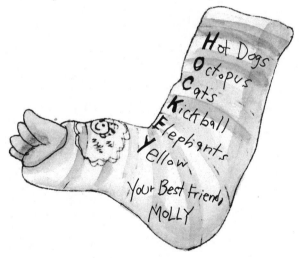

Aya read Molly's acrostic.

"It's supposed to have a topic," Aya said. "Yours is just a mish-mash. You didn't carry out any theme. What does an octopus have to do with hockey?"

Molly lowered her eyebrows. "I don't need your opinion, Aya Star*bird.*"

Aya didn't like the way Molly said the last syllable of her name. "Let's go look at the frog tank," Aya said to Florence.

After they left, Molly placed the Magic Marker back on my desk. "I suppose you hate me, too," she sighed.

"No, I don't hate anybody." Then I asked, "Do you?"

Molly paused as she looked over at Florence and then back at me. "I'm trying not to. Are you still mad at me?"

"I'll get over it," I groaned. "Maybe . . . when I'm forty!"

I wanted to rub it in. It was a perfect

time for her to apologize. But saying "I'm sorry" was never easy for Molly.

"Are we still best friends?" Molly asked.

Just as I tried to move my foot, I felt a shot of pain go up my leg. Now my face was as long as Molly's.

I think we both were feeling pain.

Just different kinds.

7

Lunch with the Teacher

Five minutes before the lunch bell, Mr. Yarg came over and asked me who I wanted to eat with in the room.

Hmmmm, I thought, *which choice would really bug Molly?*

Everyone was waiting for my decision.

"Florence," I said.

Lots of people groaned. They wanted a turn to eat in the room with the teacher.

Molly sank down in her chair. If she was

mad before, she was really mad now. Her eyes looked like BBs aimed at me.

I did what I had been wanting to do all day.

I shot her a raspberry. *Pflflflflflflflflflflflf.* It felt good to flutter my lips.

I could tell she didn't like it. She squeezed her hands into tight fists on her desk.

"So," Mr. Yarg said when he returned from taking the class to the cafeteria. "Shall we make it a foursome with the frogs?" He was carrying Florence's lunch tray.

I got my cold lunch and joined them at the science table next to the frog tank.

On the wall was a cool poster of a green poisonous frog with red eyeballs. I set my crutches down on the floor while Mr. Yarg got his lunch from the cabinet.

"Ahhh!" Mr. Yarg joked. "The Green Corner. My favorite place to dine!"

Florence giggled when she saw the teacher's lunch pail and thermos. A picture of Roy Rogers was on both of them.

"He's my hero," Mr. Yarg explained. "I grew up watching old-time cowboy shows on TV."

"Cool," I said, taking a bite of my peanut butter and Fluff sandwich. We watched the teacher take out his sandwich, four cookies and an orange.

"Excuse me," a voice said from the doorway.

We turned and looked.

It was Molly. "I forgot my lunch," she said.

I gave her the eagle eye. I knew what Molly was up to. She just wanted to spy on us.

We watched her rush into the room, bump into the garbage can and tumble onto the floor.

Mr. Yarg got up right away. "Are you okay?"

Molly moaned, "I can't move. I think I . . . might have broken . . . my leg."

I covered my eyes. *What an act,* I thought. Molly was just faking it.

"Can you stand?" Mr. Yarg asked.

Molly got up and limped around. "It hurts to walk."

"Well," Mr. Yarg said, "you might as well go get your lunch and join us."

Molly raced over to her desk. By the time she remembered to hobble, it was too late. The teacher noticed.

"On second thought," he said, "I think you can make it back to the cafeteria. I'm glad you're okay."

Molly put her head down as she walked out of the room. I could tell she was embarrassed. She didn't look at anyone. When she got behind the door, she stopped to spy on us. I know because I spotted her green shoelaces in the crack of the door.

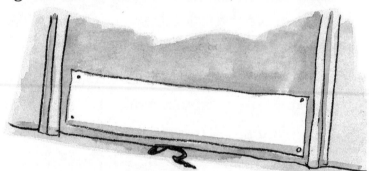

She was eavesdropping.

"Maybe Molly can have a turn to eat up here tomorrow," Florence suggested.

"That's a nice idea," Mr. Yarg replied. "Molly is lucky to have a friend like you."

When I looked again, the green shoe-laces were gone.

"Now," Mr. Yarg continued. "Why don't we ask each other a question that we'd really like to know about one another. Morty, you can go first."

Mr. Yarg chewed on some lunch meat as he waited for me to say something. I knew it was salami because I could smell the spices.

"Well," I said. "I'd like to know why Florence never told anyone she was such a great skater."

Florence thought about it as she picked up a chicken nugget and dunked it into some ketchup. "Probably because my mom told me if you're really good at something, you don't have to tell people that you are. They'll find out themselves."

"And," Mr. Yarg added, "it's because

51

Florence is very modest. Remember Wilbur in *Charlotte's Web*? How humble he was?"

When I nodded, Florence's face turned as red as her cherry Jell-O.

"Your turn, ma'am," Mr. Yarg said. "Ask a question."

Florence did.

It was a big one.

"Are your parents divorced? Mine are. It's kind of hard. I just see my dad on Sundays."

"My parents aren't divorced," I answered.

"Mine are," Mr. Yarg said.

We both looked at the teacher. It was really neat having such a personal conversation with him.

"They got divorced when I was seven. And it was hard for me, too. But you know what? I found out they both still loved me just as much. I lived with my mom during the week, and visited Dad on the weekends. I don't live with either of them now."

Florence smiled like she understood.

I crunched on a carrot and thought about things.

"My turn," Mr. Yarg said. "Because you're both mathematicians, I have a special question."

He got twenty pennies out of the gallon jar that was next to the tank. "I'm giving you each ten pennies. Watch how I am arranging them . . . in a perfect triangle.

"Now," he said. "See if you can turn this triangle upside down by moving just three pennies."

Florence moved her tray. I moved my brown bag lunch aside. We both studied the pennies carefully. In less than a minute, Florence's triangle was upside down.

She didn't blurt out "I got it!" She just sat back and waited for me to get mine.

It took me two extra minutes. "Okay, I got it, too!" I said.

"Whoa! You two are star skaters AND star mathematicians!" Mr. Yarg exclaimed. "Most kids don't get it that fast."

Mr. Yarg slapped us five.

Later that day during math, Mr. Yarg gave everybody the ten-pennies problem. He said Florence and I could be helpers.

Molly didn't even try. She just folded her arms and steamed. She was still mad. What Florence said at lunch didn't even make a difference.

That did it!

I leaned on my crutches and whispered,

"You know what, Molly? You could learn something from Florence. She's the best skater in this class, but she never brags about it. She won't even race you to prove it. She's humble, like Wilbur. You? You have to make the most points in everything. You have to be in the spotlight all the time. I'm tired of it."

There!

It all came out.

Just like my cat . . . when he threw up his food this morning. Everything was out there!

All of a sudden, Molly didn't look so mad.

She just looked *sad.*

8
Saturday Hockey

Saturday morning, Mom drove me to the Hilltop Ice Rink. After we parked, we walked across the lot. I managed to walk pretty well with my crutches. I had four days' practice. My armpits were feeling a bit sore, but that was okay. I was happy to have someplace to go.

When we got inside the rink, I saw some repairmen working on the sound system. The loudspeaker was making all kinds of crazy noises. Finally a voice said, "Test-ing, testing, testing," and the screeching stopped.

The eight- and nine-year-old players were already warming up on the ice. They were all wearing blue-and-yellow Hilltop jerseys.

Florence came running over to meet me. "Hi, Morty. Your clipboard is on the bench, and your Hilltop hockey jersey is, too."

"Cool! See you later, Mom!"

After Mom waved good-bye, Mrs. A led me over to the bench. "Flo can show you how we chart the goals, assists and blocks for each player. I'm glad you can be part of the team."

"Me, too, Mrs. A," I said.

When Molly skated by with Vincenzo, she had her head down. She didn't say hello. But Vincenzo did. "Hey there!" he called. "We're Squirts."

Florence and I waved back. Eight other kids skated by. "There's lots of people here I don't know," I said.

"They're from East and South School," Florence explained. "That big kid with the buzz cut is Mason. He's a good goalie."

As I watched him put on his helmet, I took a deep swallow. *I could have been a goalie, too,* I thought.

I watched Molly skate by a second time. She got to wear all that neat equipment— the helmet, face mask, mouthpiece, shoulder pads, rib pads, thigh pads, knee pads, shin guards, skates and gloves!

When everyone arrived, Coach Tucker blew his whistle to call the team together. I liked the way he skated around the players and came to a full stop just by turning his skates. Little bits of ice sprayed in the air when he did that.

When everyone was listening, he gave a

pep talk. "Hockey is a team sport. The most important stats that I look at are ASSISTS. You see a guy open, you send him the puck, and he scores." When he caught Molly's and Aya's eyes, he said it again. "You see a girl open, you hit her the puck, and she scores. It's teamwork! I don't care who makes the most points. I care about kids working hard whether it's on defense, blocking goals, stealing pucks or looking

for the open man. TEAMWORK wins games. Now, let's do it!"

The first warm-up drills were fun to watch. The players skated across the ice and slid on one knee for a while. Then they skated and slid on both knees. Molly slid farther than anyone else. She even outslid Mason.

"That drill helps them practice getting up when they fall in a game," Florence explained.

"Hey," I said, "how come you're not out there playing hockey with Molly?"

"My mom wants me to train for figure skating only. It's hard to do both. She knows that. She used to be on the United States Olympic skating team. She didn't win any medals or anything, but she competed."

"Wow! No wonder your mom's such a good teacher."

Florence nodded.

The next drill, Coach Tucker put five tires down the middle of the ice. "Okay, kids," he said. "I want you to skate around these tires as you move to the other side."

Swish! Swish! The players skirted in and around the rubber obstacles.

Vincenzo skated right into the first tire. Molly passed him up, laughing. After Vincenzo held up a fist, he decided not to skate with Molly anymore. He skated with Aya.

Later, the coach removed the tires and brought in a pail of pucks. I watched him dump them. They looked like black raisins on the ice.

"Okay, hit 'em back and forth with a partner," Coach Tucker said. "Keep your eye on the puck, and work on your quickness."

When Vincenzo and Aya started slapping the puck back and forth, Molly realized she had lost her partner. I bet she wished she hadn't laughed at Vincenzo.

My favorite exercise was the weave drill. That's when Florence and I started our charting. A player raced across the ice with two other teammates. They worked on changing positions and hitting the puck back and forth. When they got close enough, they tried to hit the puck into the small netted cage on the ice.

BLAM!

The goalie held up his big mitt.

"That one got blocked!" I said.

"I told you Mason was good," Florence

replied. "He works real hard at defense. Look! Here comes Molly's group."

We watched Molly pass the puck to Vincenzo. Vincenzo passed it to Aya. When Aya hit it back to Molly again, Molly raced toward the goal. She was in her "I'm gonna score first" mode. Just as Molly was about to slap the puck into the net, the sound system made another crazy noise.

Screeeech!

As Molly jerked back, her hockey stick hit

the puck the opposite way, over to Vincenzo. He was wide open for a perfect shot.

SLAP!

Vincenzo hit the puck into the net for a score.

"YAHOO FOR MOLLY!" the coach yelled. "You just earned a great assist!"

Florence jumped up and yelled, "GOOD TEAMWORK!"

I forgot how angry I was with Molly and started clapping, too, as Molly and Vincenzo circled back around the ice. When Molly looked over, she seemed surprised to find us rooting for her. After all, she wasn't the one who scored. Vincenzo was.

"ONE POINT FOR VINCENZO, AND ONE POINT FOR YOU, MOLLY!" Florence called out.

Molly gave us a weird look and then skated over to the coach. "You get a point for an assist?" she asked.

"You sure do!" Coach Tucker answered. "An assist counts just as much as a goal in our record books."

"All right!" Molly exclaimed. Then she skated off. Her smile was so wide I could see it through the holes in her face mask.

As we charted the blocks, assists and goals, we cheered on the kids we knew. I had to admit, Molly was the most fun to watch.

She raced across the ice like she was Wayne Gretzky. Her eye was always on the puck. When she fell on the ice, she never cried about it. She just got right back up again.

"How many points did you get for Molly?" I asked when practice was finally over.

"Ten!" Florence said. "Five for goals and

five for assists." Then she held up five fingers and waved them at Molly. "YOU HAD THE MOST ASSISTS!" Florence yelled.

Florence and I started to chant, "Go Molly! Go Molly!"

The next time Molly skated by our bench, she waved her hockey stick. "Hey, Morty and Flo," she called, "thanks for rooting for me."

Coach Tucker blew his whistle. "Okay, kids!" he said. "Everyone gather over here for a team picture."

We watched the ten players make two perfect rows in the middle of the ice. The tall kids stood in the back row holding hockey sticks. Molly kneeled in the middle with a chalkboard that said *HILLTOP FLYERS*.

"Wait a minute!" Molly said, holding up her gloved hand. "We need Morty and Florence."

"Of course," the coach replied. "Our scorekeepers!"

Florence and I exchanged a smile. It felt good to be considered part of the team.

As I got up on my crutches, Molly dropped her sign and raced over to help. Just as we were taking our first step onto the ice, the coach screamed, "Wait a minute! You don't want to break your other leg, Morty. Stay put! We'll take our picture over there, on the edge of the ice."

As the team skated over to us, Molly quickly whispered something in my ear. "I'm sorry, Morty. I'm real sorry about what happened. Are we still friends for life?"

"Yeah," I said, "for life." Then I looked down at my cast and groaned, "But with you for a friend, who knows how long that'll be?"

When Molly broke out laughing, I did, too.

"Hey, cut it out, you guys!" Mason said as he slapped his hockey stick on the ice. We were surrounded by the team now. "No smiling," he barked. "We're tough! We're the Hilltop Flyers!"

And that's when Molly and I looked as **mad** as we could be!

CLICK!

HILLTOP HOCKEY
SQUIRTS DIVISION 8-9
"FLYERS"

Solution to the puzzle on page 54:

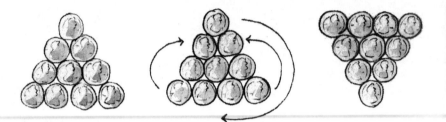